THIS CANDLEWICK BOOK BELONGS TO:

_____

_____

_____

Henry & the Crazed Chicken Pirates

Carolyn Crimi

illustrated by John Manders

Candlewick Press

enry and the Buccaneer Bunnies lived on an island. They spent their days reading books they had collected over the years, shooting one another out of cannons, and swinging from the masts of their ship. They were a happy bunch.

Until one day when Henry found a mysterious message in a bottle.

Henry couldn't stop thinking about the note.

"We might trip over coconuts while we're trying to run away from the enemies," he said to his father, Barnacle Black Ear, in the midst of a heated game of coconut bowling.

"Stop worryin' about that old note," said Black Ear.

"What if they come while we're sleeping?" Henry asked Calico Jack Rabbit, who was busy swabbing the deck.

"That's enough chitter chatter out of you!" said Calico Jack.

"What if a parrot poops in my eye and I can't see them coming?" Henry fretted to Jean LeHare while he helped him dig for lost treasure.

"Don't be a blubbering fool," said Jean LeHare. "Relax, matey!"

But Henry couldn't relax. He read everything he could.

Soon Henry had enough information to start his own book, which he called *Henry's Plan for Impending Danger from the Unknown Enemy Who Wrote the Scary Note.* He spent every spare moment working on it.

"Quit wastin' yer time on writin'! Leave that to the professionals," Black Ear bellowed every time he saw Henry making notes.

But Henry kept writing.

One day, on the other side of the island, Henry saw a strange sight. Floating down from the sky was a hot-air balloon filled with crazed chicken pirates.

Henry raced back to find the other Buccaneer Bunnies. "I just saw a hot-air balloon filled with crazed chicken pirates!" Henry cried.

Black Ear laughed. "Yer talkin' crazy again, Henry!"

"Maybe ye should get yer eyes checked!" said Jean LeHare.

"Or eat more carrots!" said Calico Jack.

But Henry knew what he had seen, so he started working even harder on his book, testing and retesting his strategies.

"Henry, what happened?"

"My Parrot-Poop Helmet slipped down over my eyes, and I tripped!" said Henry.

"Henry, what's wrong now?"

"I was trying to attach a ladder to my lookout," said Henry.

"Henry, what are you
doing down there?"

"I was trying to hop over my crazed-chicken-pirate trap," said Henry.

"Stop writin' that blasted book of yers, or I'll toss
it into the sea!" growled Black Ear.

But Henry kept writing.

One morning Henry heard a funny sound coming from the ship.
He paged through his book until he found the chapter he
was looking for:

FUNNY SOUNDS
Coming from the
SHIP

If funny sounds
should start
coming from the
ship, investigate
without being
seen or heard.

Henry grabbed his spyglass and quietly climbed up to his lookout.

The other Buccaneer Bunnies were tied up while a gang of crazed chicken pirates rummaged through the ship.

"Get the ropes!"

"Find their loot!"

"Spill yer guts or we'll throw ye to the sharks!"

"Uh-oh," said Henry. He knew that he would need to think fast and act bravely.

"The problem," thought Henry, "is that I do not really think fast, and I am not brave at all."

Then Henry remembered something from his chapter "Facing the Enemy": *When the enemy is nearby, pretend to be brave.*

Henry put on his Parrot-Poop Helmet (which always made him feel brave), grabbed a coconut, and hopped to the ship.

"Pretend to be brave," he whispered.
He adjusted his Parrot-Poop Helmet
and tossed the coconut onto the ship.

"Hey, you crazed
chicken pirates!
You're nothing
but a bunch
of dopey
drumsticks!"

Seconds later they came dashing down the gangplank,
clucking and flapping with gusto.

"Get him!" shouted the largest one.
Henry hopped faster than he ever had before.

"BOWK! Come back here!"

"Stop that hippety-hopping!"

"BOWK BOWK!"

Henry kept going until he reached his crazed-chicken-pirate trap.
Just before he was about to fall in, he hopped to the right.

"Suffering scallywags!"

"Crikey!"

"BOWK!"

Every last crazed chicken pirate tumbled into the trap.

"You blimey bunny!" they shouted. "Get us out!"

"Sorry," said Henry. He scampered back to the ship
and untied the crew.

"Three cheers for Henry!" they cried. They toasted him with cups of coconut milk.

"Anything in yer book about what to do with a bunch of crazed chicken pirates?" asked Black Ear.

"As a matter of fact, there is," said Henry.

Afterward, Henry sat down in the sand and started to write.

"What book are ye writin' now, Henry?" asked Black Ear.

Henry smiled. "I think I'll call it *Henry and the Crazed Chicken Pirates*."

To Deb and John, my Buccaneer Buddies
C. C.

For Anne Bonny, Mary Read, Grace O'Malley,
Lady Killigrew, and Carolyn
J. M.

Text copyright © 2009 by Carolyn Crimi
Illustrations copyright © 2009 by John Manders

First paperback edition 2010

Library of Congress Cataloging-in-Publication Data

Crimi, Carolyn.
Henry and the Crazed Chicken Pirates / Carolyn Crimi ; illustrated by John Manders. — 1st ed.
p. cm.
Summary: When the Buccaneer Bunnies receive a note from an unknown enemy, Henry researches
and writes a book called "Henry's Plan for Impending Danger from the Unknown Enemy Who Wrote
the Scary Note," which helps him when the enemy finally arrives.
ISBN 978-0-7636-3601-2 (hardcover)
[1. Rabbits — Fiction. 2. Books and reading — Fiction. 3. Authorship — Fiction. 4. Pirates —
Fiction. 5. Chickens — Fiction.] I. Manders, John, ill. II. Title.
PZ7.C86928Hec 2009
[E] — dc22   2008025454

ISBN 978-0-7636-4999-9 (paperback)

10 11 12 13 14 15 16 CCP 10 9 8 7 6 5 4 3 2 1

Printed in Shenzhen, Guangdong, China

This book was typeset in Myriad and Blackfriar.
The illustrations were done in watercolor, gouache, and pencil.

Candlewick Press
99 Dover Street
Somerville, Massachusetts 02144

visit us at www.candlewick.com

Carolyn Crimi, aka the Pirate Queen, is the author of numerous books for young readers, including *Where's My Mummy?* and the award-winning *Henry and the Buccaneer Bunnies*, both illustrated by John Manders. About *Henry and the Crazed Chicken Pirates*, she says, "While I don't have long floppy ears or a pronounced overbite, Henry and I are kindred spirits, who love books and carrots!" Carolyn Crimi lives in Illinois.

John Manders—thief, pirate, rogue, and children's book artist—has illustrated several picture books for children, including *Henry and the Buccaneer Bunnies, Where's My Mummy?, The Perfect Nest,* and *Minnie's Diner: A Multiplying Menu.* He says, "I began my nautical career with my faithful parrot, Sherman, plundering merchantman and man-o'-war alike. From piracy, it was a small step to children's book publication." Today John Manders lives in Pennsylvania, far from the ocean's beckoning waves.